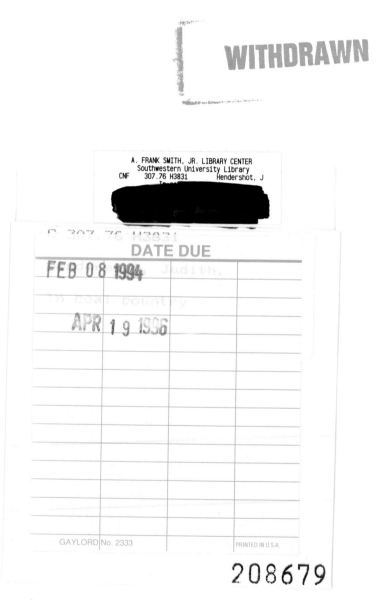

IN COAL COUNTRY

by Judith Hendershot · illustrated by Thomas B. Allen

Alfred A. Knopf 🐕 New York

THIS IS A BORZOI BOOK
PUBLISHED BY ALFRED A. KNOPF, INC.

Text copyright © 1987 by Judith Hendershot
Illustrations copyright © 1987 by Thomas B. Allen
All rights reserved under International and Pan-American Copyright
Conventions. Published in the United States by Alfred A. Knopf, Inc.,
New York, and simultaneously in Canada by Random House of
Canada Limited, Toronto. Distributed by Random House, Inc., New York.
Manufactured in the United States of America
Designed by Eileen Rosenthal

2 4 6 8 0 9 7 5 3

Library of Congress Cataloging-in-Publication Data
Hendershot, Judith. In coal country. Summary: A child growing up in a
coal-mining community finds both excitement and hard work, in a
life deeply affected by the local industry. [1. Coal mines and
mining—Fiction] I. Allen, Thomas B., ill.
II. Title. PZ7.H3787In 1987 [E] 86–15311
ISBN 0–394–88190–7 ISBN 0–394–98190–1 (lib. bdg.)

The illustrations for this book were done in pastels and charcoal
on Mi-Teintes papers and reproduced in full color.

For my parents, Fred and Della Demkowicz,
who were coal country kids before me
J.H.

For Laura and Hilary,
for their love and patience
T.B.A.

Papa dug coal from deep in the earth to earn a living. He dressed for work when everyone else went to bed. He wore faded denims and steel-toed shoes and he walked a mile to his job at the mine every night. He carried a silver lunch bucket and had a light on his miner's hat. It was important work. He was proud to do it.

In the morning I listened for the whistle that signaled the end of the hoot-owl shift. Sometimes I walked up the run to meet Papa. He was always covered with grime and dirt, but I could see the whites of his eyes smiling at me. He let me carry his silver lunch bucket.

When we got home, Mama took the number three tub from where it hung on the back porch and filled it with water heated on the huge iron stove. She draped a blanket across one corner of the kitchen, and Papa washed off the coal dust. We got a bath only on Saturdays, but Papa had one every day. Then Papa went to bed and we went to school.

We lived in a place called the Company Row. The ten white houses sat in a straight line. They were built by the people who owned the Black Diamond Mine. Two miners' families lived side by side in each two-story house. Seventy-five children lived and played there in the row. We had many friends.

Outside, our houses never looked clean or painted. Coal was burned in the furnaces to heat the houses and in the stoves to cook the food. The stove fires sent smoke and soot up the chimneys. The smoke had a disagreeable smell, and something in it made the paint peel off the houses. Tiny specks of soot floated out and covered everything.

Our coal camp was called Willow Grove. The houses were huddled in a hollow between two softly rising hills. In the spring the hills were covered with lady's-slippers and yellow and white violets. Mama always had a jar of spring flowers on the kitchen table. Weeping willow trees lined the banks of the creek that flowed behind the Company Row.

The water in the creek was often black. The coal was dragged out of the mine in small cars pulled by mules. Then it was sent up into a tall building called the tipple, where it was sorted and washed. The water that washed the coal ran into the creek, and the dust from the coal turned it black as night.

Papa sometimes worked at the picking table on the tipple to sort out rocks from the good coal. After it was sorted, the good coal was dumped into railroad cars waiting under the tipple. The rest of the stone and dirt was hauled away to a gob pile. There were gob piles all over Willow Grove. The kids from the row ran to the tops of the piles to play king of the mountain.

Sometimes a gob pile caught fire. It smoldered for a long time, maybe for days, and it smelled awful. When the fire went out, the stone and ash that was left was called red dog. Our roads were made of the sharp red-dog stone.

Trains moved the coal in cars from the mine to power plants and steel mills on the Ohio River. The train tracks ran alongside the Company Row. We watched from the porch swing as the engineer worked his levers to guide the train, blowing clouds of hot white steam on the tracks. One engine pushed and another pulled as many as one hundred cars at a time. The houses shook as the trains rumbled by.

The coal cars moved all through the day and into the night. Sometimes in the middle of the night we heard the clang of steel as the cars were hitched to the engine. Often the load was too much for the engine. It groaned. The tracks creaked. The wheels screeched as the brakeman spread sand on the rails to get the cars moving. Then the train began to move very slowly, and we could hear the wheels straining a slow "Chug-a-chug, chug-a-chug." Later, in the distance, the engine's whistle moaned a familiar cry. "Whoo-whoo."

In the morning we took buckets and gathered the lumps of coal that had rolled off the cars in the struggle the night before.

The vibration of the trains often made the rails on the tracks come apart. When that happened, the paddy man came to repair the tracks. He rode a flatcar, which he pedaled by himself. While he worked to replace the spikes in the rails, the paddy man sang:

> *"Paddy on the railroad,*
> *Paddy on the sea.*
> *Paddy ripped his pants,*
> *And he blamed it on me."*

Mama worked hard like Papa. She planted our garden and she canned vegetables for the winter. She stored her quart jars of beans and tomatoes and peas in the earthen room in the cellar. Every other day Mama baked her special rye bread in the oven of the iron stove. We often ate the bread right out of the oven with fried potatoes and sliced tomatoes.

Washing the clothes was a long, hard job. We carried the wash water from the pump down by the creek. Mama heated the water in a copper boiler on her huge stove. She scrubbed the clothes on a washboard with a stiff brush. Her hands were red and wrinkled when she was finished.

In the summer, when it was hot, the Company Row kids often climbed the hills above the grove. We cooled ourselves by standing under Bernice Falls. The water flowed from a natural spring on the ridge above. It was cool and clean and it tasted so sweet.

We walked the red-dog road to the Company Store. Anything the miners' families needed, from matches to pongee dresses, could be found there. Every payday Papa treated us to an Eskimo Pie.

The Company Row kids played hopscotch in the dirt. Our favorite game was mumbletypeg. In the evenings we built bonfires along the creek and roasted potatoes on willow sticks.

In the autumn the hills were ablaze with color. We gathered hickory nuts and butternuts and dragged them home in burlap sacks. Papa shelled them and spread them on the porch roof to dry. Mama used the nutmeats in cookies at holiday time.

In the winter we climbed from the hollow to Baker's Ridge. Our sleds were made from leftover tin used for roofs, and we rode them down through the woods by moonlight. When the black creek was frozen, we shared a few skates and everyone took a turn. When we got home, we hung our wet clothes over the stove to dry and warmed ourselves in Mama's kitchen.

Christmas in the row was the best time of the year. Papa cut a fresh tree up on the ridge, and we pulled it home on a tin sled. Mama placed a candle on the end of each branch. The tree was lighted once, on Christmas Eve. Papa spent the whole day basting the roast goose for Mama. Our stockings bulged with tangerines and nuts and hard cinnamon candies. The house smelled of Christmas tree and roast goose and all the good things that Mama had made. No whistle called Papa to the mine. Everything felt so special. And it was.

*J*udith Hendershot comes from a family of coal miners. She was born and raised in Neffs, Ohio, less than a mile from Willow Grove, where her father and both grandfathers worked in the mine. She has drawn from her parents' memories of growing up in Willow Grove, as well as from her own, to write *In Coal Country*. She earned a degree in education from the University of Akron and now teaches language arts to the sixth grade in Brimfield, Ohio. She and her husband have three grown children and one grandchild. *In Coal Country* is her first book.

*T*homas B. Allen grew up in Nashville, Tennessee, and studied painting at the School of the Art Institute of Chicago. He has illustrated several books for children, including *Blackberries in the Dark* by Mavis Jukes, and *Tom Sawyer* and *Huckleberry Finn* for the Franklin Library. He is currently Hallmark Distinguished Professor in the Department of Design at the University of Kansas in Lawrence, where he lives with his wife and daughter.

About the illustrations for *In Coal Country* he says: "They are the most honest I've ever done. Though I didn't grow up in a coal town, the pictures are out of my own experience of growing up during the Depression, the grandson of a railroad man."